Kipper had a box and a bin.

Kipper got in his jet . . .

... and put on the lid.

"This jet is cool," said Kipper.

"Off I go," he said.

The jet shot off.

boom
boom

It shot out of the room.

"I will loop the loop," said Kipper.

The jet did six loops.

"I will go to the moon," said Kipper.

"I can get to it soon," he said.

I can shoot to the moon.

The jet got to the moon.

But the moon bugs ran up.

"Yuk," said Kipper. "Moon bugs."

"Shoo, get off," said Kipper.

"Did I nod off?" said Kipper.
"Yes," said Mum. "Get up to bed."